All profits from the sale of this book will be allocated

to those affected with Multiple Sclerosis with the hope that

within our lifetime MS will stand for "Mystery Solved."

Acknowledgements

Kristin Blackwood

Mike Blanc

Jennie Levy Smith
Trio Design & Marketing Communications Inc.

Dennis Roliff

Dr. Janet Stadulis

Paul Royer

Kurt Landefeld

Sheila Tarr

Michael Olin-Hitt

Julianne Stein

Larry Chilnick

Karen Strauss
Strauss Consultants

www.VanitaBooks.com

What Pet Will I Get?

Vanita Oelschlager

illustrated by

Kristin Blackwood

This book is dedicated to
my granddaughter Annalexis
and
all my other grandchildren.

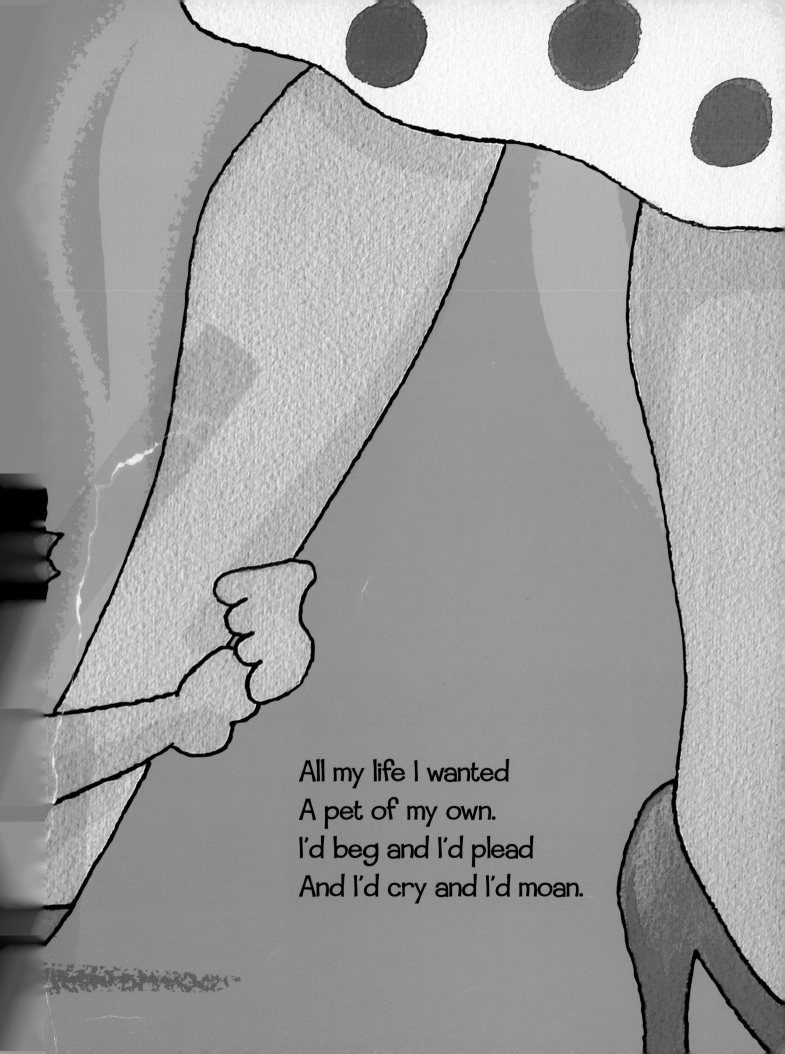

All my life I wanted
A pet of my own.
I'd beg and I'd plead
And I'd cry and I'd moan.

I said I would feed it,
Whatever it ate,
In a stable or cage,
A dish or a plate.

I'd brush it and clean it
And pet it all day.
I'd stop all my moaning,
If I'd get my way.

I even bartered
And said I would clean
All my dirty, stinky socks
In the washer machine.

I said to my mother,
I'd make breakfast in bed
If she got me a pet,
And she FINALLY said,

"I'll go to a store
Where pets can be bought,
And I'll get you a pet
Right there on the spot."

I've pictured this day
So long in my head.
I'm so excited
I make my own bed!

My Mom might get anything,
Either little or big.

A dog? A cat?
A pot belly pig?

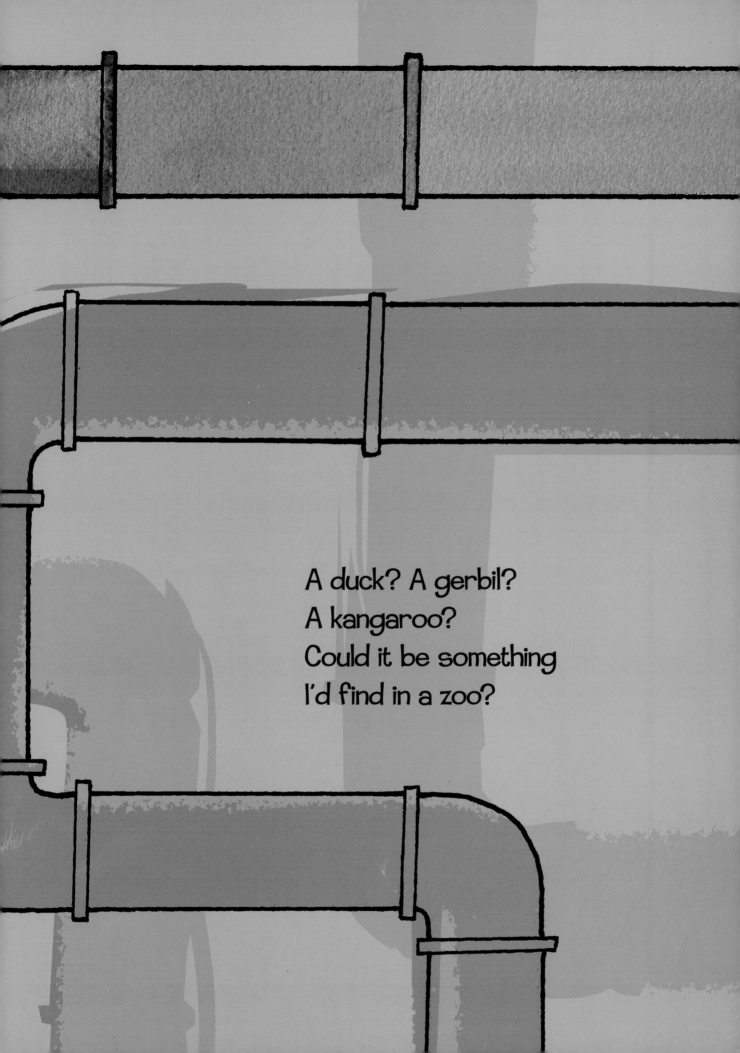

A duck? A gerbil?
A kangaroo?
Could it be something
I'd find in a zoo?

Mom's at the pet store.
That's where pets are bought.
She might buy a parrot,
But probably not.

I hear my mom coming.
Oh, what will it be?
It will be a pet
For just only me.

I see my mom bouncing
Her way up the drive.
And what is that with her?
Is it even alive?

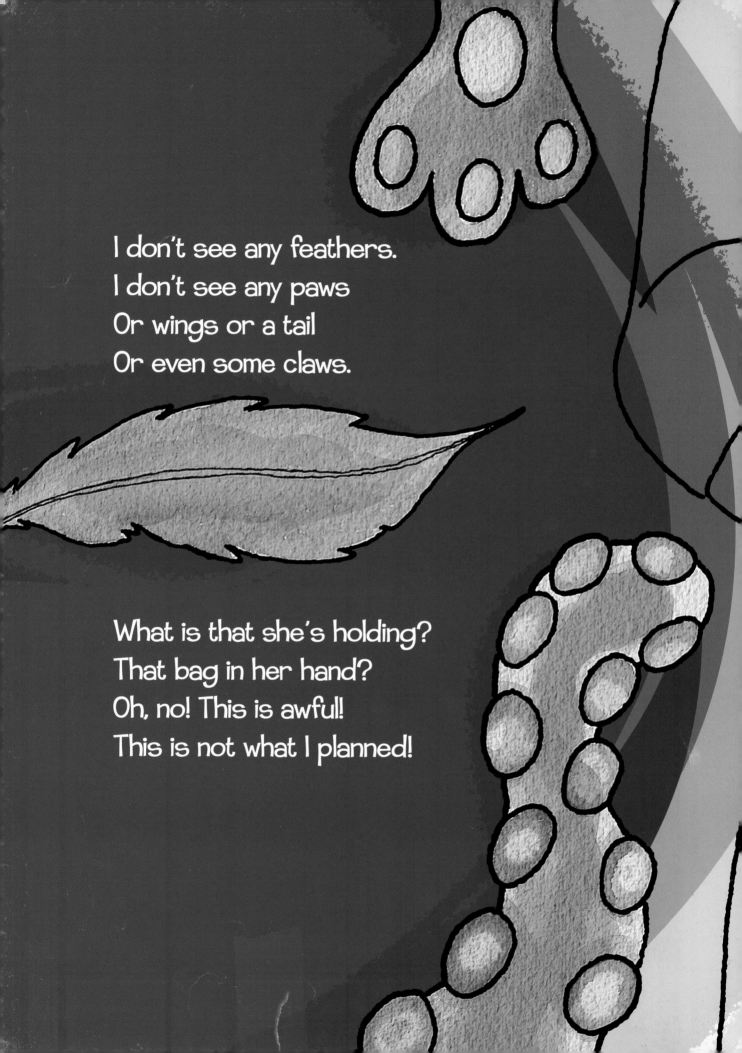

I don't see any feathers.
I don't see any paws
Or wings or a tail
Or even some claws.

What is that she's holding?
That bag in her hand?
Oh, no! This is awful!
This is not what I planned!

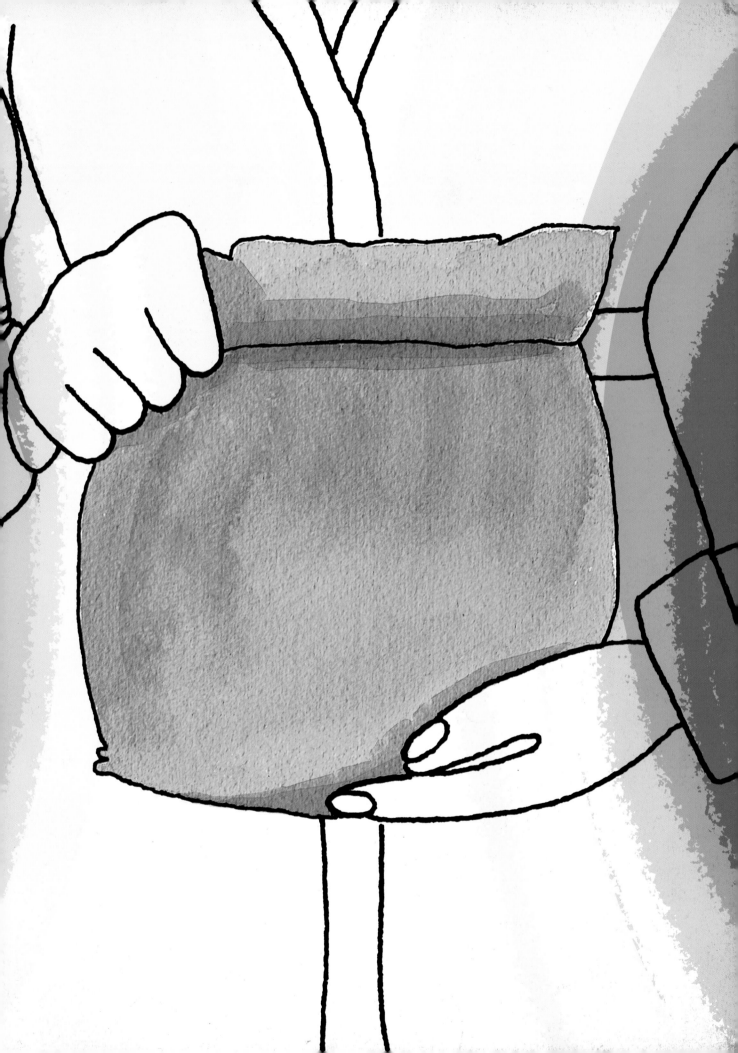

I hoped she would bring me
A cute little puppy.
But she marched through the door
With a stupid old guppy.

A guppy is the smallest
Of very small fish.
He's so small and so nothing,
He'd get lost in a dish.

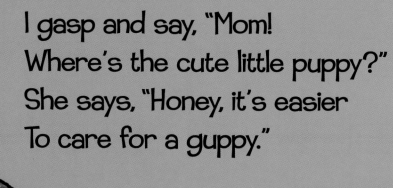

I gasp and say, "Mom!
Where's the cute little puppy?"
She says, "Honey, it's easier
To care for a guppy."

"Okay, then," I say.
"A kitten, then. Please?"
She says, "Cats are messy
And end up with fleas."

I tell her I hoped for
A llama at least.
She says she can't handle
Taking care of a beast.

I don't stop there,
"What about an iguana?"
My mom says, "Not unless
We're in Tijuana."

I look in her pocket.
I'm hoping to find
A rat or a gerbil,
Or a mouse of some kind.

I just keep on saying,
"This isn't a pet"
My mom's had enough.
"Well, it's all that you'll get."

I go to my room,
And sit on my bed.
I put down my fish,
And I lower my head.

I'm feeling so bad,
I'm starting to cry.
Of all things, a guppy!
Oh, why, why, why, why?

I look at that fish.
He looks back at me.
I really can't say
I like what I see.

I start my computer,
And get on the 'Net.
I type the word "guppy"
To see what I'll get.

And there on my monitor
What do I find?
Guppy fish hits
Of every kind.

I couldn't believe it.
Could this really be true?
There are guppy sites everywhere -
Way more than a few.

My favorite site
Is a cool guppy blog -
The World Guppy Championship
Is this year in Prague!

I go back to my guppy.
He's starting to swim.
I stick in my finger,
I'm playing with him.

I open the food jar
Mom stuffed in my hand.
He darts to the surface
And eats on command.

At night when the moonlight
Hits my guppy just right,
I'm telling the truth,
He's a beautiful sight.

First thing in the morning,
Before Mom is awake,
I ask my guppy
"What plans should we make?"

I see that he likes me.
That's hard to resist.
My hopes for a puppy
No longer exist.

I've fixed up his bowl,
He lives like a king.
He stops swimming to listen
When I start to sing.

I bring in some marbles
To brighten his bowl.
I put in a seashell
With a peek-a-boo hole.

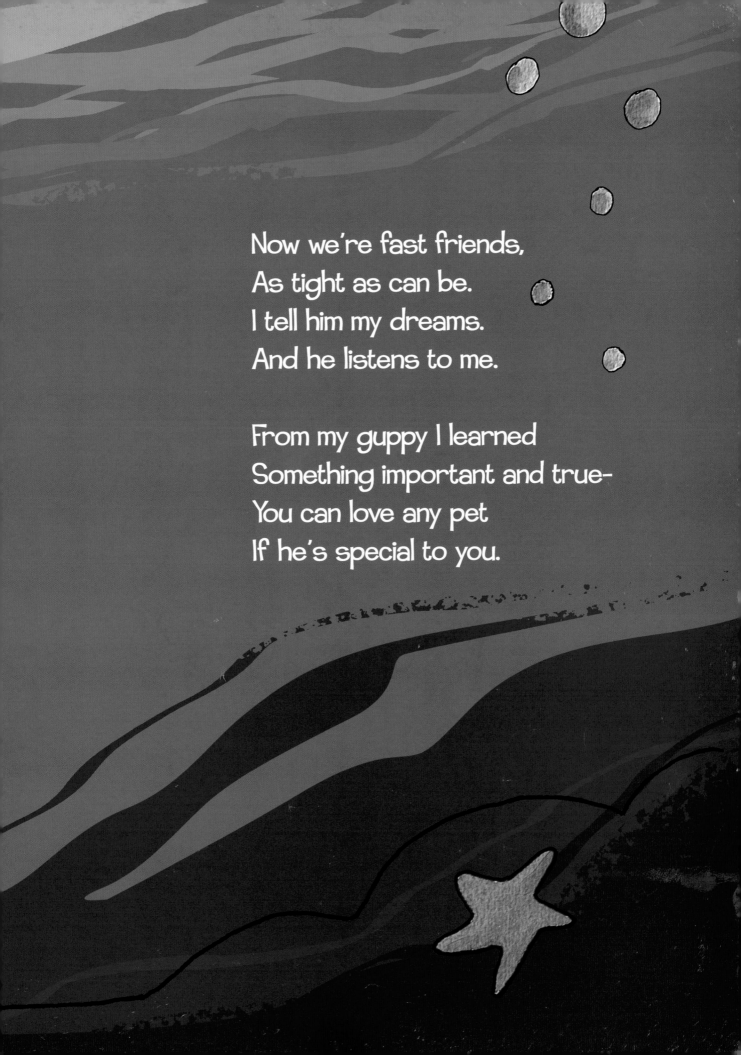

Now we're fast friends,
As tight as can be.
I tell him my dreams.
And he listens to me.

From my guppy I learned
Something important and true-
You can love any pet
If he's special to you.

Kristin Blackwood is an experienced illustrator whose other books include: *My Grampy Can't Walk,* *Let Me Bee,* and *Made In China.* She has a degree from Kent State University in Art History. In addition to teaching and her design work, Kristin enjoys being a mother to her two daughters. She also enjoys working with her mother, who is also the author.

Vanita Oelschlager is a wife, mother, grandmother, businesswoman, philanthropist, former teacher, current caregiver, author, and poet. She is a graduate of Mt. Union College in Alliance, Ohio, where she currently serves as a Trustee. Her latest book, *My Grampy Can't Walk,* is an uplifting story about the unique relationship between her husband, Jim, who has multiple sclerosis and their grandchildren. Vanita is also Writer In Residence for Literacy Programs at the University of Akron.

Kristin's illustration is a blending of techniques, beginning with traditional line art drawings and water media on Arches® 300lb cold press watercolor stock. The paintings were then photographically captured in digital format. Color backdrops were created using Corel® Painter™, and Adobe® Photoshop®, computer software for digital illustration. The lively result is a playful and satisfying journey through *What Pet Will I Get?*.